DABBLING DOEZEE

To my nieces and nephews C.J., Lydia, Wesley, and Wren
—Kimberly Kennedy

For dearest Lanna, an angel in heaven
—Tracy Herrmann

This edition published by Fabula Publishing
Redmond, WA
www.doezee.com
Printed in Canada by Friesens

Library of Congress Control Number: 2014932886
ISBN: 978-0-9915194-0-8

DABBLING DOEZEE

by Kimberly Kennedy
illustrated by Tracy Herrmann

Doezee dabbles.

Her head goes under the shallow water and her tail tips up in the air.

Then she stirs the mud to find her lunch.

Doezee's friend Rudy dives.

Rudy swims under the water to look for food.

They tell stories and trade treasures after they dabble and dive.
"I'll swap you a fish for a bug," Rudy offers.

"Yuck, you know that I don't eat stinky fish," Doezee responds.
They gab and jabber as friends often do.

Every day Doezee dabbles while Rudy dives.

Today Doezee hears growling and snarling.

"Oh no!" she says when she sees the predator gang.

The coyote, the fox, and the weasel have Rudy trapped.

"You're going to be this pack's snack," the coyote says
and smacks his lips.

Rudy is smart enough to do what diving ducks do.

He dives under the water.

Rudy pops up out of the gang's reach.

Doezee is happy that Rudy is safe, but she is scared.

She also wants to be safe from the coyote, the fox, and the weasel.

She wants to become a diving duck too.

Doezee starts by trying to look the part.

She paints her bill blue like Rudy's bill.

She paints her feathers red
like Rudy's feathers.

She glues on a tall tail like Rudy's tail.

Doezee goes to the tip-top of the tallest rock.

She poses like a diver then over she goes.

She flips and rolls.

Her feet flail and feathers fly.

WHACK

Then she hits the water on her back.

"Doezee, why do you want to dive?
No one dabbles better than you," Rudy says.

"Diving kept you safe from the gang,"
Doezee explains.

Rudy remembers how frightened he
had been and he wants to help his friend.

"I'll teach you to dive," Rudy says.

Rudy shows Doezee how to dive.

He tucks his short wings against his body.

He goes all the way under the water.

He moves his head, neck, and body up and down.

He kicks his big feet.

Rudy comes back up with a fish in his mouth.
CHEW, GOBBLE, SWALLOW.
"Gross. You're eating fish again," Doezee complains.

Rudy laughs and replies, "I'm not teaching you to dive for food.

I'm teaching you to dive so you don't become food.

Now you try. Touch the bottom of the lake."

Doezee squeezes her wings in close.

She holds her breath and goes under the water.

She tries to move up and down, up and down.

She tries to kick her feet.

Doezee flips and rolls and then flops back onshore.

"My feet are too small. My wings are too big.

How can I stay safe if I can't learn to dive?"
Doezee sniffles.

"You aren't safe. Dabblers can't dive.

That's why we will munch on puddle duck today," the wicked weasel says.

The fox lunges at Doezee.

Doezee flies straight up in the air.

The coyote pounces at Rudy.

"Do not hurt my friend!"

Doezee shouts as she swoops down at the coyote's head.

As soon as Rudy's feet touch the water,

Doezee yells, "Dive, Rudy, dive!"

Rudy dives and then he quickly swims down.

Doezee and Rudy meet behind the cattails far away from danger.

"Doezee, you flew straight up. I have to run on water before I can fly, but not you," Rudy says.

"I didn't know that I could fly up with one flap of my wings,"
Doezee says, and dances about.
Doezee now knows how to stay safe from the gang.

That night Doezee and Rudy tell their friends about escaping from the coyote, the fox, and the weasel.

Doezee tells the story as seen from up above.

Rudy tells the story as seen from below.

They talk about wings that are perfect for flying.

They talk about feet that are too big and feet that are too small.

And they talk about friends helping friends, which is the part that matters most of all.

AUTHOR'S NOTE

Doezee is a mallard. She is a dabbler. Dabbling means that when a duck looks for food in the water, the head goes underwater and the tail tips up in the air. Dabbling ducks often look for food on top of or under shallow water. Dabbling ducks usually have larger wings than diving ducks. Dabblers can fly straight up with one flap of their wings. A female duck is called a duck. Doezee is a dabbling duck.

Rudy is a ruddy. He is a stiff-tailed diver. Diving ducks go all the way under the water to look for food. Some diving ducks do not walk well on land because they have bigger feet set farther back on their bodies. Sometimes diving ducks patter on the water surface to build up speed so that they can fly. A male duck is called a drake. Rudy is a diving drake.